W9-BRD-145

First published in the United States in 2019 by Sourcebooks, Inc.

Text © 2018 by Eloise Greenfield

Cover and internal design © 2019 by Sourcebooks, Inc.

Cover images and illustrations © 2018 by Ehsan Abdollahi

Sourcebooks and the colophon are registered trademarks of Sourcebooks, Inc.

All rights reserved.

The characters and events portrayed in this book are fictitious or are used fictitiously. Any similarity to real persons, living or dead, is purely coincidental and not intended by the author.

Handmade and hand-colored paper was used to create the collage art.

Published by Sourcebooks Jabberwocky, an imprint of Sourcebooks, Inc.

P.O. Box 4410, Naperville, Illinois 60567-4410

(630) 961-3900

Fax: (630) 961-2168

sourcebooks.com

Originally published in 2018 in the UK by Tiny Owl Publishing, London.

Library of Congress Cataloging-in-Publication data is on file with the publisher.

Source of Production: Shenzhen Wing King Tong Paper Products Co. Ltd.,
Shenzhen, Guangdong Province, China

Date of Production: January 2019

Run Number: 5013952

Printed and bound in China.

WKT 10 9 8 7 6 5 4 3 2 1

THINKER

MY PUPPY
POET
AND
ME

words by

ELOISE GREENFIELD

pictures by

EHSAN ABDOLLAHI

sourcebooks
jabberwocky

NAMING ME

They brought me from the neighbor's house
and put me on the floor,
they talked about their love for me,
and I thought, "More! More! More!"

I kept my eyes from opening,
I kept my voice on mute,
until I heard somebody say,
"Let's name him something cute."

My eyes popped open, and I said,
"Uh-uh! No way! No way!
I'm deep and I'm a poet. No!
A cute name's not okay."

The boy called Jace said, "You're a poet?
I'm a poet, too.
We'll name you 'Thinker,' yes, I think
that *that's* the name for you."

They named me Thinker, and I knew
this was the place to be.
A place that named me Thinker
was the perfect place for me.

WELCOME PARTY

At my welcome party,
Dad sang, Mom spoke,
Kimmy danced, and Jace
told a joke.
I said,
"Thank you, thank you,
to you four,
I'll love you all
forevermore,
this family means so much
to me,
I hope you like my poetry.
The end."

TWO POETS TALKING

Thinker to Jace:
If I'm not reciting a poem,
my tongue won't let me talk,
I can only bark.
But barking can't say much,
just ruff-ruff, "I'm glad to see you"
or howl "Oh-woooo, I'm scaring
youuuu," and bow-wow
for everything else.
Words, though, can say anything
I want to say, in the way
I want to say it.

Jace to Thinker:
When I recite my poems,
I make music. I say the words
fast or slow, high or low,
I stop and I go, almost
like singing, making
word-music.

TELL ME, JACE

You've been in the world
a long, long time,
so tell me, Jace, please
tell me,
why cold, cold water
turns to ice,
why some folks are mean
and some are nice,
why puppies and people
like to race,
why babies like
to pat my face.
Tell me, Jace.

JACE'S ANSWER

I don't know, Thinker, I don't know,
I'm only seven, got a long way to go.
Let's keep learning what life is all about,
and pretty soon, we'll have this world
all figured out.

JACE WON'T LET ME GO

I want to go to school with him,
but when I try to get on the
yellow bus, he says, "No, no, no,
you can't go!"
I whine and whine, but I know
what he's thinking. He thinks
I might recite a poem,
and his friends will say
he's a weird kid, with a weird pet.
But I won't talk, *I won't*.
I'll just do some of the things
he told me about.
I'll sit at a desk, and raise my hand,
I mean my paw, raise my paw,
and wave it at the teacher.
I'll eat my puppy biscuits at the
lunch table and get in line
and go outside and slide,
and race and chase.
But Jace says, "No, No, No, No,
No!

YOU! CAN'T! GO!"

KIMMY

Kimmy likes to play ball,
throw it, kick it, sit on it,
bounce on it. When she gets up,
I pounce on it, kick it, move it
with my nose. I love the sound
of Kimmy's laughter. One day soon,
I'll make up a poem about it.

MY BROTHER

My twin brother lives across the street,
once in a while, we meet to eat,
he listens to me, lets me talk,
doesn't complain and doesn't balk,
just waits and listens like a friend,
and barks a period at the end.

IN THE PARK

Let's take a walk
around the park,
but please don't forget
that you have to bark.
No matter what you
want to say,
just watch, think, and bark,
okay?

IN THE PARK 2

Not many people in the park,
nobody near enough to hear me,
if I say a poem or two.
So I do.

WEATHER HAIKU

Cool out here today,
but I don't need my sweater.
My hair is enough.

BIRDS FLY

Birds fly,
flap their wings,
and touch the sky.
Why can't I just
wag my tail
and sail?

YOU CAN GO

Guess what, Thinker?
Tomorrow is Pets' Day at school,
and you can go.
You won't be the only one,
we're going to have a lot
of fun.
You won't talk,
will you?

PETS' DAY

All the pets are here.
The teacher is teaching,
the children are at their desks,
and I am sitting on the floor
beside Jace's feet.

I remind myself of the rule:
watch, think, bark,
watch, think, bark.
No poems. No talk.
But I am sad.
Who am I, if I'm
not myself?
Who am I?

And the next thing I know,
I'm jumping up and running,
running to the front
of the room, and I start
reciting a funny poem.

I sneak a look at Jace, and
I'm surprised. He's laughing.
So I keep talking, and then,
the cat starts singing opera,
and the frog is walking upside
down

and the three goldfish
are dancing in the fish tank,
and the canary is fanning
the teacher with his wings.
The children are laughing,
the teacher is laughing,
and best of all,
Jace isn't mad at me.

THAT'S MY PUPPY

I thought Thinker might
shame me, but I am proud
of him. I pat him on the back,
and I say,
"You're cool, Thinker.
Keep on being your
cool self."

So Thinker starts to rap,
and we walk out of the school,
and on down the street.
Going home.

THINKER'S RAP

Walking out the school door,
didn't come to stay,
didn't mean to talk, but
did it anyway.
My friend, Jace, beside me,
walking to my beat,
children, pets, and grown-ups,
filling up the street.
Stopping all the traffic,
going down the hill,
nothing else is moving,
everything is still.
Mom and Dad and Kimmy
giving us a cheer,
standing on the front porch,
watching as we near.
Going in the house now,
going to close the door.
Got to say goodbye now,
please don't ask for more.
Going in the house now,
my good friend and I,
got to say goodbye now.
Goodbye, goodbye, goodbye.
GOODBYE!

ELOISE GREENFIELD

I enjoy reading and writing different kinds of poetry, but the kind I write most often is free verse. The word "free" doesn't mean that the poet is free to write just anything. A poem still must be shaped, but I need to shape my poems using the word-music I hear in my head.

Whenever I write a poem using a shape invented by another poet, I have to be sure that the shape and my words can work well together. Otherwise, it would feel wrong, like trying to make a square painting fit into a round frame.

About rap, some people don't believe that it is real poetry. I say that it *is* poetry, absolutely. Like other kinds of poetry, it uses meaning, rhythm, rhyme, hints, humor, repetition, and wordplay to make it come alive.

I hope you have enjoyed meeting Jace and Thinker and that, if you have not already done so, you will take some time, now and then, to write a poem or two.

Eloise Greenfield

With love, to the children of the world.
—E.G.

For all the mothers and fathers who
taught their children how to love.
—E.A.

ELOISE GREENFIELD was born on May 17, 1929, in Parmele,
North Carolina, and grew up in Washington, DC, where she still lives.
She has received many awards and honors, including the Coretta Scott
King—Virginia Hamilton Award for Lifetime Achievement and, for the body
of her work, the Award for Excellence in Poetry for Children from the
National Council of Teachers of English.

EHSAN ABDOLLAHI is an illustrator and teaches at Tehran Art
University in Iran. Ehsan creates handmade and hand-colored paper in his
collages, which are inspired by the environment, fabrics, and clothes of the
people he meets. Ehsan has also illustrated *When I Coloured in the World*
and *A Bottle of Happiness* for Tiny Owl.